Lilibet &
The Creature

PHAEDRA MOON

Art by Norville Parchment

FIRST EDITION

Once there was a little girl named Lilibet who lived all alone in a small white cottage. The sun always shone on the cottage, which sat within the gates of a pretty pastel garden, nestled in the center of a vast golden field.

Within her home were gleaming oak shelves stuffed with books and adorned with lovely trinkets, crystals and figurines. Colourful paintings hung on the walls, and Lilibet loved to gaze into the images — pictures of strange animals, summer picnics and swirling dancers. She would search the faces of the women and girls and try to see herself, for she had never seen a mirror. Although she lived alone, it had never occurred to her to feel lonely, because her books were full of beloved stories and poems with all kinds of interesting people to know.

Lilibet spent her sunny days reading on a mossy patch in her garden, surrounded by pink tulips and bellflowers and tidy rows of fox gloves. She would lose herself as she wandered through the pages, finding friends and enemies and sometimes even glimpses of herself.

So, she read and dreamed, and learned many of the secrets of the heart from her books, knowing that someday she would grow up and become ready to leave her little cottage and explore the great wide world full of love and sorrow and dreams.

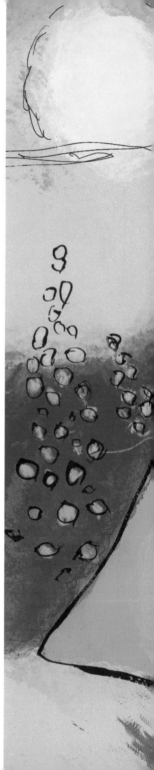

One day, after a thousand days of golden sunshine, as Lilibet sat reading in her garden, a drop of wet sky fell down and plopped right on the page in front of her. She scowled her very first scowl and looked irritably up at the sky, only to find that it seemed full of water, and the drops continued to tumble down on her, wetting her face, flattening her curls and smearing the ink on the page in front of her.

Soon, the rain became
so heavy that Lilibet ran
inside, into the sanctuary
of her cottage of trinkets
and stories. She didn't
wrap herself in a blanket
or a towel, but instead sat
dripping and trembling
by the window. As she
watched a strange dark
glow transforming her
garden, she suddenly had a
strange twisting feeling in
the pit of her stomach, as
if some new creature had
come alive.

When the rain began to settle, Lilibet crept outside to explore the transformed world, and found that, in a place where there once had been a soft mossy crevice, there was now a clear silver pool. She approached it cautiously, feeling the creature churn inside of her.

When Lilibet leaned over and peered into the
glassy surface, a shocking reflection stared back
at her. She jumped back, and then took a deep
breath, and looked again...but the mocking image
remained the same. Looking back at her from the
silver pool was not a little girl at all, but a woman.

Lilibet fell to the ground and wept.

Who was this woman on the surface of the water? She didn't feel like a woman, and indeed, did not want to be a woman at all. She had read about many women in her stories and poems, and had never recognized herself in any of them. How had she become a woman without knowing it? And what had happened to the years that lay in between?

She lay her body down beside the pool and thought these troubling thoughts for a very long time. The sun fell and rose again, and then it fell and rose again. She longed for her familiar stories and her pretty trinkets, but was afraid that they had changed with the rest of the world.

When she finally rose to go back into the cottage, she
noticed some curious plants had encroached into her
garden. Next to the demure patch of bellflowers, a
swell of tall crimson poppies, ragged tiger lilies, and
wild roses of red and orange were spreading across the
garden, scaling the white gates,

and creeping out into the vast golden field. There
was something about the look of these flowers that
disturbed her, although they were quite beautiful. She
eyed them suspiciously as she passed by, and the creature
in her stomach grew warm.

Lilibet was pleased to see her books lay unchanged on their shelves. She picked up her favorite, sat in her comfiest chair, and opened to the first page. But just as she feared, the story seemed different. The parts that had once only been sad now broke her heart, and there were strange dark shadows hiding in even the sunniest parts. The creature slowly stirred, warming her from inside, and she grew unsettled. She scowled her second scowl at the page and then jumped to her feet and hurled the book against the door. It fell with a thump and a flutter. Her breathing was hard, and the moment closed in on her.

S uddenly, there was a firm
knock at the cottage door.
She moved towards it bravely and
opened it just a crack. Standing
on the threshold was a stranger.
The grey of their eyes was the
same dark glow that had overcome
Lilibet's world. She let the door
swing open and stood with
her arms crossed in front
of her chest.

The stranger was beautiful and frightening, with a serious face and strong arms that held out a brazen bouquet of tiger lilies, poppies and a fierce tangle of wild roses.

They stood in silence,
with the thorny
flowers between
them, but her arms
remained tightly
crossed.

"**Those aren't the kind of flowers I like."**

Lilibet said crossly. But her creature disagreed. The creature began to move up her spine like a corkscrew, and it pulled her towards the flowers, which she reached for and buried her face into, breathing so deeply that the colours flooded her body.

As her hand wrapped around the flowers, tiny thorns pierced into her flesh and warm trickles of blood pooled in the creases between her fingers and dampened the cluster of stems. Her hand grew hot, and the creature purred.

Lilibet stepped out to join the stranger with a sense of fear and wonder, and their eyes met with mysterious understanding.

Together they stepped
over her favorite book that
lay splayed open on the
floor,across the cottage
doorway, past the mingled
garden, out of the gates
and into the vast
golden world.

For Eva & Maceo